Zoom Squirrel

Zing Squirrel

Flappy Squirrel

Norman

Research Rodent

Wonder Squirrel

Wink Squirrel

Klink Squirrel

HYPERION BOOKS FOR CHILDREN / *NEW YORK*

Look, **Zip Squirrel**! I found a **bagel of contents**!

Thanks, **Boom Squirrel**, but I'll use this **table of contents**!

TABLE OF CONTENTS

Look for the **EMOTE-ACORNS** in this story.

They pop up when the Squirrels have **BIG** feelings!

HAPPY

EXCITED

SURPRISED

NERVOUS

ENCOURAGING

FRUSTRATED

MAD

SAD

CONFUSED

FUNNY

The **BIG** Story!

Guess
WHAT!?

By **Mo Willems**

GUESS

I am going to the beach in **seven days**!

6 days to go

Squirrel friends!

Some-squirrel is going to the beach in **six days**!

Guess who?

You?

GUESS!!!

5 days to go

Going to the beach!
Yay! Yay! Yay!

♫ *Going! Going! Going!*
*In **five days!*** ♫

How—

Dance!

fun!

Dance!

Dance!

Zoomy's beach day is in **four days**!

3 days to go

Three days!

15

2 days to go

Going to the beach!
Yay! Yay! Yay!

16

Going! Going! Going! In **two days**!

Dance!

Dance!

Dance!

1 day to go

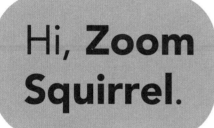

Hi, **Zoom Squirrel**.

Hi, **Wonder Squirrel**!

18

Guess what!?

I am going to the beach in **one day**!

WONDERFUL!

I **wonder** what you are going to do there.

Zoomy!

Are you ready—

to **go** to the beach?

I do **not know**.

I do not know **anything** about the beach!

That is **okay**!
We will show you what **we** **like** to do!
Squirrel-style!

Here we are at the beach!

We like playing in the sand!

Try it!

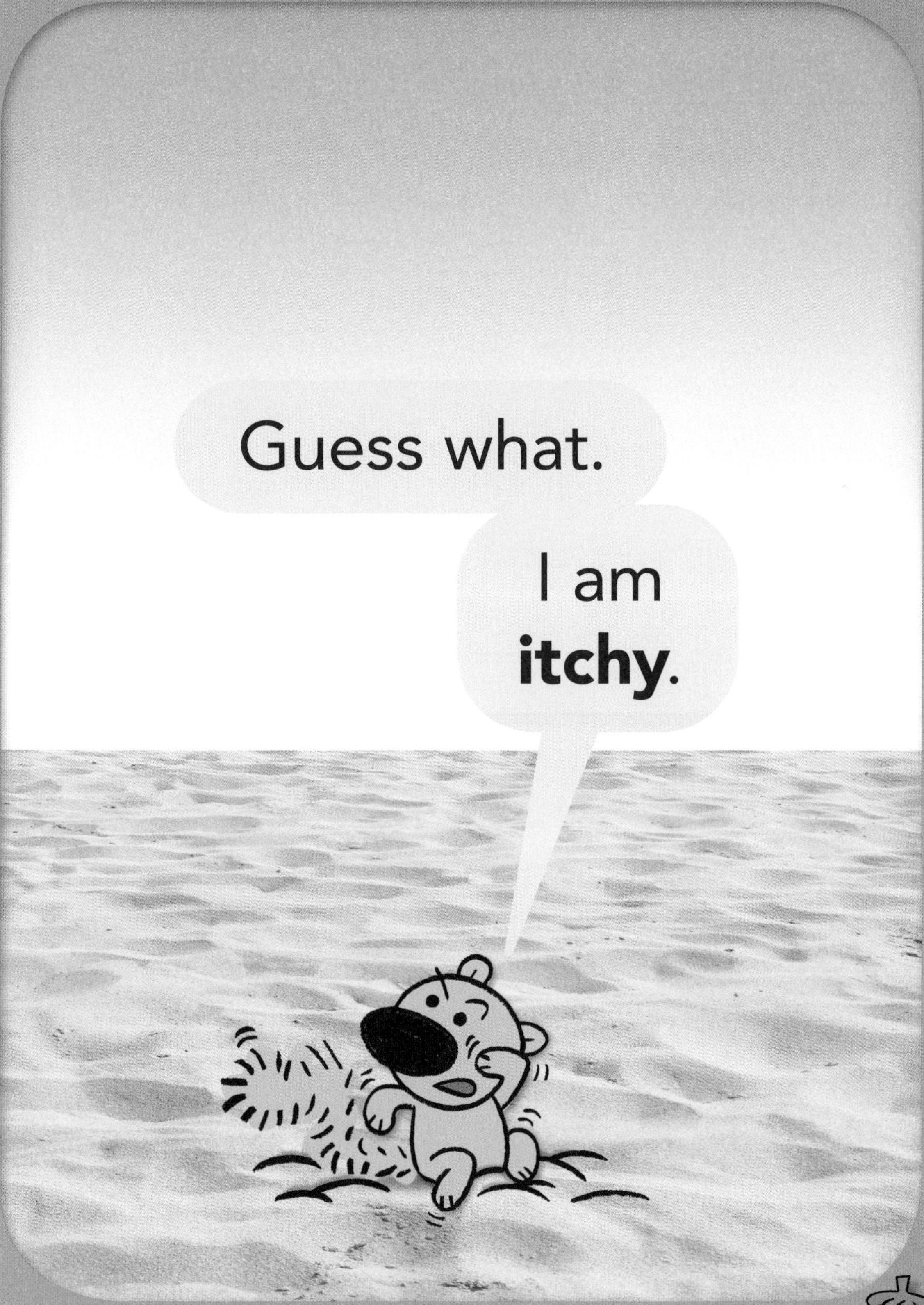
Guess what.
I am **itchy**.

Okay.

We also like playing with the **beach ball**.

Yeah!

Beach ball?

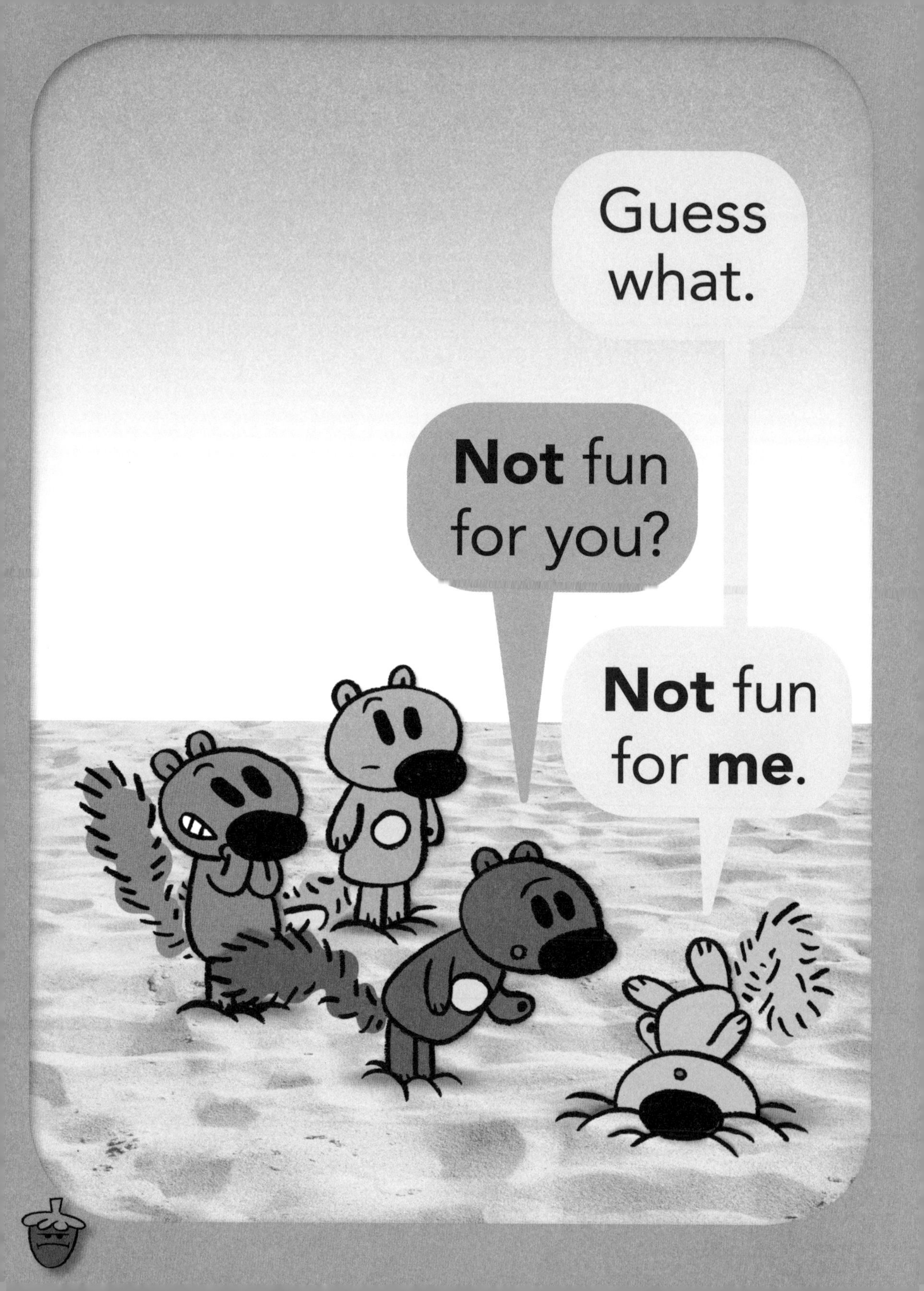
Guess what.
Not fun for you?
Not fun for **me.**

How about the **water**?
We really like playing by the water.
I will try.

Zoom Squirrel!

We want to **apologize**.

We are **sorry**.

Why?

You **did not like** the sand!
You **did not like** the beach ball!
YOU **DID NOT LIKE** THE WATER!

Yes, I had a **bad day**.

But **guess what**?

I had a **great week**!

I **sang** my beach song.

Dance! Dance! Dance!

I **danced** my beach dance.

I **counted down** my beach countdown!

I just do not like **being** there.

♪♫ Went to the beach!
Went and now I'm **done**! ♫

Went! Went! Went!
The going part was **fun**!

I **guess** we learned something this week.

Squirrels **do not know much** about beaches.

BEACH DAY!

Squirrels may not know much about the beach, but YOU can!

SEE THE SEA!

SHORE BIRDS hunt for tiny creatures hiding in the sand—when they are not running away from you!

SEASHELLS are the outer homes of animals like snails and clams.

SAND is made from worn-down rocks, minerals, and seashells. It can be white, beige, pink, red, black, or even green.

WAVES are made by wind blowing across the water. Boats and earthquakes make waves, too!

SOUND WAVES!

SQUEAK!

When you step on sand, it makes different sounds depending on the type of sand. The noise is made by grains of sand **RUBBING** together.

POP!

The bubbles popping **UP** in the sand are from air trapped below.

SPLASH!

The sound of crashing waves comes from bubbles splashing **DOWN** against the shore.

WHOOSH!

If you listen inside a **CONE-SHAPED** seashell, you'll hear an echo an echo an echo!

BEACH SQUIRRELS

Just like Zoom Squirrel, most squirrels don't like the beach. Squirrels can swim, though. They paddle with their legs and steer with their tails!

For more beach facts, visit unlimitedsquirrels.com!

It's ACORN-Y JOKE TIME!

100% CORNY!

Hi-Corn! Are you stronger than Monday?

Hey-Corn! Am I stronger than Monday? **Sure—**

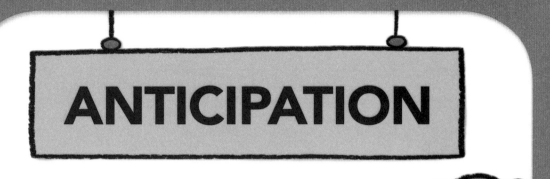

ANTICIPATION

Look! A **big word!**

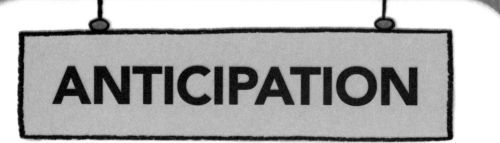

ANTICIPATION

That **is** a **big word**!

What does it mean?

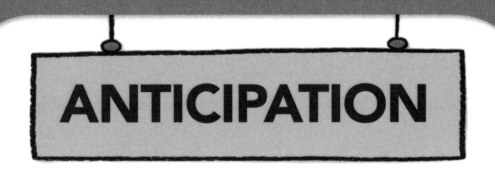

ANTICIPATION

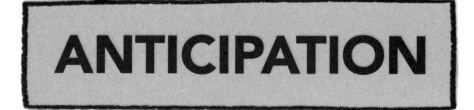

ANTICIPATION

We are **excited** to find out what that word means!

ANTICIPATION

An-tic-i-pa-tion is the excited feeling you have **before** something happens.

Like finding out what a word means!

DISAPPOINTMENT

It's **ACORN-Y JOKE** TIME!

100% CORNY!

Hey-Corn! What kind of TV did the dictionary buy?

Hi-Corn! I don't know! What kind of TV did the dictionary buy?

GUESSING GAME!

Let's play a **guessing game, Wowie Squirrel!**

Okay, **Zowie Squirrel.**

Well—

It looks like a duck.

And it **walks** like a duck.

And it **quacks** like a duck.

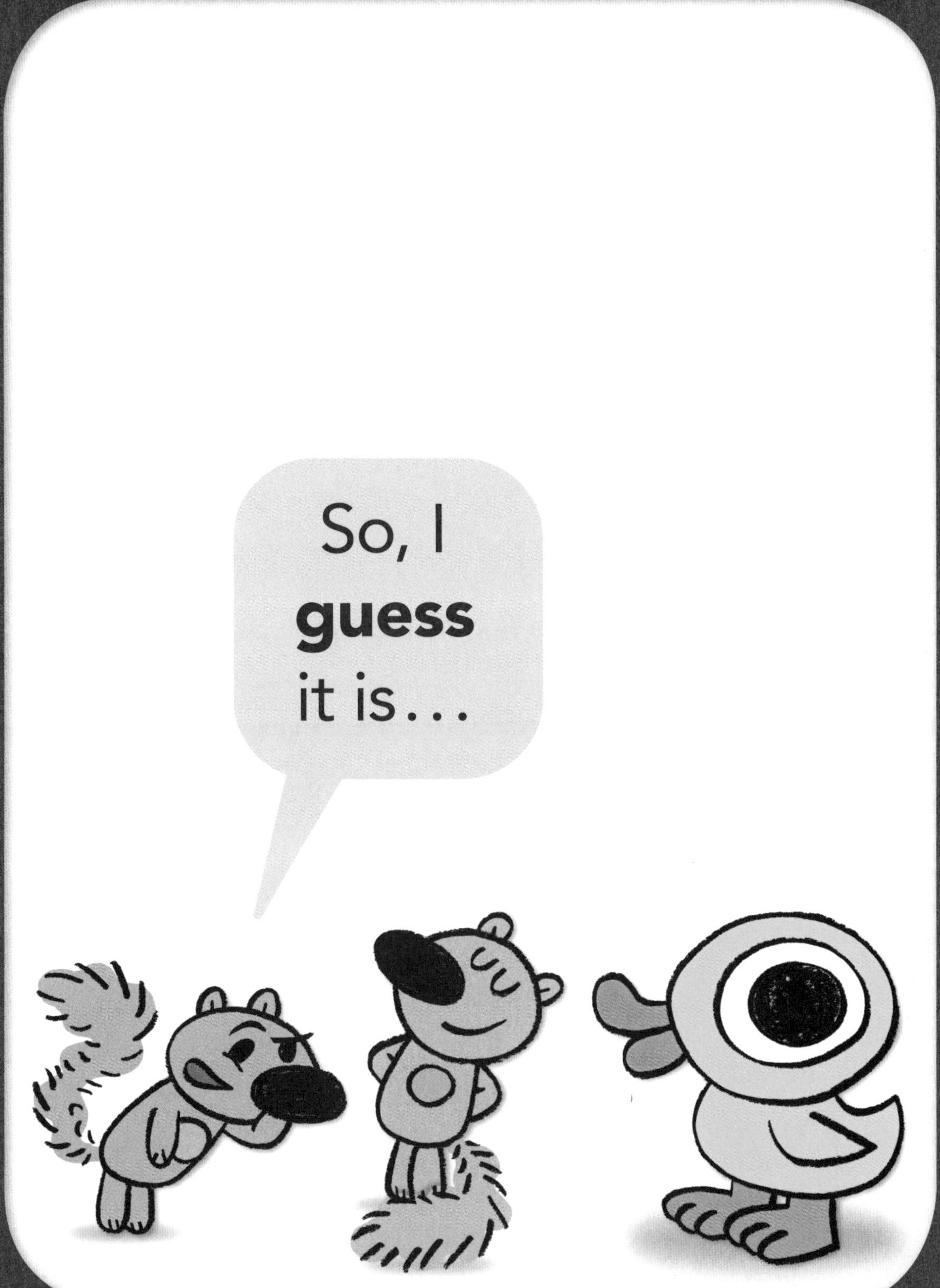
So, I **guess** it is...

It's ACORN-Y JOKE TIME!

Hey-Corn!

Hi-Corn!

12.273% CORNY!

Hi-Corn! Why is a **clock** never in a hurry?

Hey-Corn! Give me a second....Why is a clock never in a hurry?

Because it has **all the time in the world!**

You could use a **time-out**.

Text, illustrations, and music © 2021 by Mo Willems
ELEPHANT & PIGGIE is a trademark of The Mo Willems Studio, Inc.

Music by Deborah Wicks La Puma

This book is set in Avenir LT Pro/Monotype; Minion Pro, Billy/Fontspring; Typography of Coop,
Fink, Neutraface/House Industries
Stock images: Piping plover chicks with female 219076453, seashells 100511771, extreme
close-up of sand grains 199018590, magnifying glass 18879790, countdown numbers 234234281,
music notes 292583957/Adobe Stock; sandy beach 1179590641/Shutterstock

Printed in the United States of America
Reinforced binding

First Edition, October 2021
10 9 8 7 6 5 4 3 2 1
FAC-034274-21232

Library of Congress Cataloging-in-Publication Data

Names: Willems, Mo, author, illustrator.
Title: Guess what!? / by Mo Willems.
Description: First edition. • New York, New York : Hyperion Books for
    Children, 2021. • Series: Unlimited squirrels • Audience: Ages 4–8. •
    Audience: Grades PreS–3. • Summary: "Zoom Squirrel and the Squirrel pals
    are looking forward to going to the beach"— Provided by publisher.
Identifiers: LCCN 2020047866 • ISBN 9781368070935 (hardback)
Subjects: CYAC: Squirrels—Fiction. • Beaches—Fiction. • Humorous stories.
Classification: LCC PZ7.W65535 Gue 2021 • DDC [E]—dc23
LC record available at https://lccn.loc.gov/2020047866

Visit www.hyperionbooksforchildren.com and www.pigeonpresents.com

A BIG SQUIRRELLY THANK-YOU TO OUR EXPERT!

Joseph T. Kelley, professor, School of Earth and Climate Sciences, the University of Maine